This edition published by Parragon Books Ltd in 2015 and distributed by

Parragon Inc.
440 Park Avenue South, 13th Floor
New York, NY 10016
www.parragon.com

Copyright © Parragon Books Ltd 2012-2015

Written by Lulu Frost
Illustrated by Lorna Brown and Fran Brylewska

ISBN 978-1-4748-1428-7

Printed in China

The Moonlight Tooth Fairy

PaRRagon

Bath • New York • Cologne • Melbourne • Delhi
Hong Kong • Shenzhen • Singapore • Amsterdam

Twinkle was a tooth fairy.

Every night, she flew from house
to house collecting the teeth that
children had left under their pillows.

Each time she took a tooth, she
slipped a shiny coin in its place.

Before she flew away,
she always whispered,
"Sweet dreams!"

Twinkle loved to
make people happy.

But Twinkle often felt lonely.

She saw sisters sharing a bedroom.

She saw friends sleeping over.

She saw moonlit moths playing together.

"I wish I had
a friend, too,"
she thought.

One night, Twinkle came to
Abigail's house. She flew in
through the open window and
tiptoed onto Abigail's pillow.

Carefully, Twinkle reached
for Abigail's tooth, and put
it in her tooth fairy pouch.

She pulled out
a shiny coin ...

But, suddenly, Twinkle felt that somebody was watching her. She turned around. A fairy face was staring at her in the moonlight!

"Silly me," thought Twinkle. "It's only a picture!" Then she noticed that there were fairies everywhere! Twinkle was so amazed that she didn't look where she was flying ...

Ouch! Twinkle bumped into a
bookshelf and dropped the coin.
It clattered onto the floor and
rolled behind the cupboard.
The noise woke Abigail.

Twinkle knew that the Tooth
Fairy should never be seen.

With a flit of her wings, she
darted behind the curtain.

Abigail sat up in bed and
rubbed her sleepy eyes.

Twinkle peeped out from behind the curtain. She watched Abigail put her hand under her pillow. The tooth was gone, but there was nothing in its place!

"Poor Abigail," thought Twinkle. "If only I had another coin." But her pouch was empty.

Abigail's eyes filled with tears. "Maybe the Tooth Fairy thinks I haven't been good," she said.

"Oh no!" Twinkle cried out. "That's not true!"

Abigail spotted Twinkle and
gasped with amazement.

"Oh dear," thought Twinkle. "Now
I've broken the Tooth Fairy Rule!"

Twinkle knew she had been seen,
so she fluttered over to the bed.
She gave Abigail her tiny hankie.

"I'm sorry, Abigail," she whispered. "I lost your coin."

Abigail gazed at the moonlight glistening on the fairy's silvery wings and smiled.

"Am I dreaming?" she asked.

"No, you're not dreaming!" laughed Twinkle.

Twinkle explained what had happened. She watched Abigail gazing at her wings and had an idea. "Would you like me to give you a wish instead of a coin?" she asked.

Abigail's eyes sparkled with excitement. "Oh, yes please! There's something that I've always wished for," she said shyly.

"Yes?" asked Twinkle.

"I wish to be a fairy, just like you!"

Twinkle waved magic into the room.

Suddenly, Abigail felt herself shrinking. Her pajamas turned into a beautiful dress made of petals, and little rosebuds blossomed in her hair. Something tickled her shoulders ...

"Look!" she cried. "I'm growing wings!" Sure enough, Abigail was soon as tiny as Twinkle, with a matching pair of shimmery wings.

Gently, Abigail opened her
wings and gave them a
flutter. "Will you teach me
how to fly?" she asked.

"It's easy!" said Twinkle.
"Hold my hand ..."

And up they rose!

Twinkle and Abigail flew to the mirror so
Abigail could admire her new wings. Then
Twinkle led Abigail out into the moonlit yard.

Twinkle and
Abigail flew
high and low.

They danced
in and out of
the trees, and
fluttered from
flower to flower.

"Look at me!" cried Abigail, as
she skimmed the starry pond.

They swooped and looped and soared.
"I love being a fairy!" Abigail said.

"It's much more fun with two," laughed Twinkle,
happily. At last, she had a real friend of her own.

Soon it was time for Abigail to go back to being a little girl. "Thank you for making my wish come true," she said to Twinkle.

"You've made my wish come true, too!" replied Twinkle.

"Come back soon," said Abigail with a sleepy yawn.

Twinkle promised. "Just put your next lost
tooth in this fairy pouch, and I'll be back as
quick as the moths in the moonlight," she said.

And as she flew away, she whispered ...

"Sweet dreams, my fairy friend!"

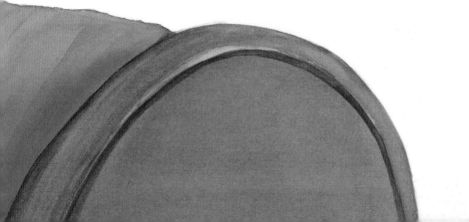